The Frog Who Was Afraid to Hop

by Liza Charlesworth

ISBN: 978-1-338-67429-3

Art Director: Tannaz Fassihi; Illustrated by John Lund
Copyright © 2020 by Liza Charlesworth. All rights reserved. Published by Scholastic Inc.

10 9 8 7 6 5 4 3   68   20 21 22 23 24 25 26/0

Printed in Jiaxing, China. First printing, June 2020.

Frank Frog was a nice green frog
who lived in a nice blue pond.

Frank was good at swimming.
Swim, swim, swim!

Frank was good at croaking.
Croak, croak, croak!

Frank was good at everything
except hopping.
"Hop!" said his frog friends.
But Frank was afraid.

"What if I hop too high?"
"What if I hurt my leg?"

"What if I jump up and bump my head?" he cried.

Frank was so afraid to hop
that he never even tried.

One day, two kids came to the pond.
"Look at that nice green frog.
I will catch him!" said the boy.

Frank was afraid.
He was so afraid that...

HOP!
He hopped away.

Then he hopped again
and again and again.

HOP, HOP, HOP!

Frank hopped so far away,
the boy could not catch him.

"Hooray!" said his frog friends.
"You finally learned how to hop."

After that, Frank was the best hopper
in the whole pond—
especially when kids came by.